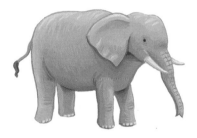

# Note to parents, carers and teachers

*Read it yourself* is a series of modern stories, favourite characters, traditional tales and first reference books written in a simple way for children who are learning to read. The books can be read independently or as part of a guided reading session.

Each book is carefully structured to include many high-frequency words vital for first reading. The sentences on each page are supported closely by pictures to help with understanding, and to offer lively details to talk about.

The books are graded into four levels that progressively introduce wider vocabulary and longer text as a reader's ability and confidence grows.

## Ideas for use

- Begin by looking through the book and talking about the pictures. Has your child heard this story or looked at this subject before?

- Help your child with any words he does not know, either by helping him to sound them out or supplying them yourself.

- Developing readers can be concentrating so hard on the words that they sometimes don't fully grasp the meaning of what they're reading. Answering the quiz questions at the end of the book will help with understanding.

*For more information and advice on Read it yourself and book banding, visit www.ladybird.com/readityourself*

Book
Band
6

**Level 2** is ideal for children who have received some reading instruction and can read short, simple sentences with help.

## Special features:

Frequent repetition of subject words and concepts

Short, simple sentences

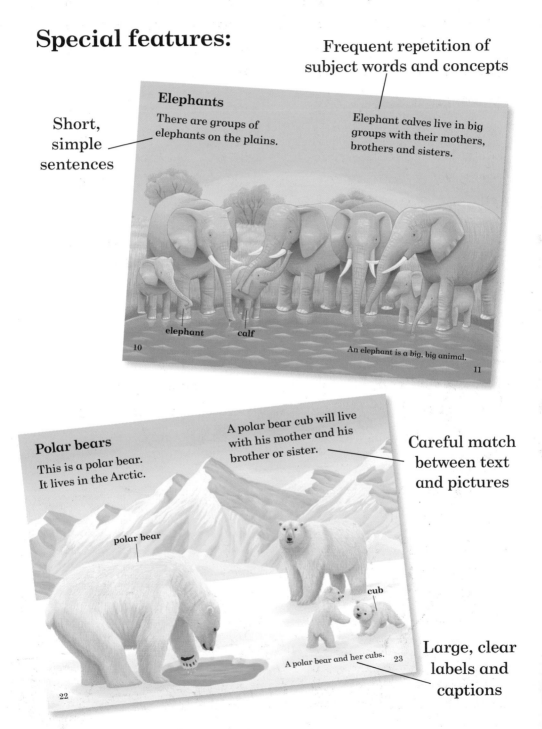

### Elephants

There are groups of elephants on the plains.

Elephant calves live in big groups with their mothers, brothers and sisters.

elephant    calf

10

An elephant is a big, big animal.

11

### Polar bears

This is a polar bear. It lives in the Arctic.

A polar bear cub will live with his mother and his brother or sister.

Careful match between text and pictures

polar bear

cub

A polar bear and her cubs.    23

22

Large, clear labels and captions

Educational Consultant: Geraldine Taylor
Book Banding Consultant: Kate Ruttle
Subject Consultant: Dr Kim Dennis-Bryan

LADYBIRD BOOKS

UK | USA | Canada | Ireland | Australia
India | New Zealand | South Africa

Ladybird Books is part of the Penguin Random House group of companies
whose addresses can be found at global.penguinrandomhouse.com.

ladybird.com

Penguin
Random House
UK

First published 2015
001

Printed in China

A CIP catalogue record for this book is available from the British Library

ISBN: 978-0-723-29510-5

# Wild Animals

Written by Monica Hughes
Illustrated by Natalie Hinrichsen

# Contents

Animals in the wild     8

Elephants     10

Cheetahs     12

Gibbons     14

Parrots     16

Fennec foxes     18

Scorpions     20

Polar bears     22

Dolphins     24

Sharks     26

Picture glossary     28

Index     30

Wild animals quiz     31

# Animals in the wild

There are many animals in the wild.

Some wild animals live in groups and some other wild animals do not.

All these animals live in the wild.

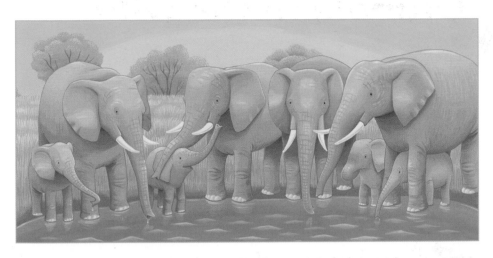

# Elephants

There are groups of elephants on the plains.

elephant

calf

Elephant calves live in big groups with their mothers, brothers and sisters.

An elephant is a big, big animal.

# Cheetahs

Cheetahs live on the plains.

Cheetah cubs live with their mother and their brothers and sisters.

cub

A mother cheetah and her cubs.

Cheetahs are big animals.

cheetah

# Gibbons

There are many gibbons
in the jungle.

Gibbons live in family groups.

mother gibbon

Gibbons go from tree to tree like this.

# Parrots

All these parrots live in the jungle.

Some parrots live in little groups. Some parrots live in big family groups.

Where is the big group of parrots?

Parrots go from tree to tree like this.

# Fennec foxes

This wild animal is a fennec fox.

It lives in the desert with other fennec foxes in a family group.

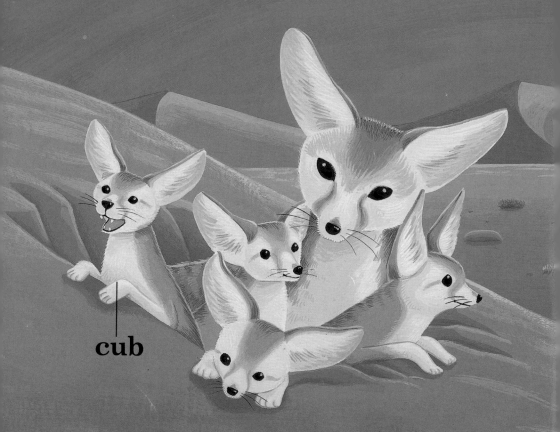

cub

The fennec fox is not a big animal.

All the group looks after
the fennec fox cubs.

fennec fox ——

# Scorpions

There are many scorpions in the desert.

A mother will look after her little scorpions.

little scorpions

Do you see the little scorpions?

**scorpion**

# Polar bears

This is a polar bear.
It lives in the Arctic.

polar bear

A polar bear cub will live
with his mother and his
brother or sister.

cub

These polar bears live in the Arctic.

# Dolphins

There are many dolphins in the sea.

These dolphins and their calves live in family groups.

calf

dolphin

Dolphins are big sea animals.

# Sharks

There are many sharks in the sea.

Some are big and some are little.

# Many sharks are big, big animals!

This shark is a little animal.

# Picture glossary

 cheetah

 desert

 dolphin

 elephant

 fennec fox

 gibbon

 jungle

 parrot

 plains

 polar bear

 scorpion

 shark

# Index

cheetahs 12

desert 18, 20
dolphins 24

elephants 10

fennec foxes 18

gibbons 14

jungle 14, 16

parrots 16
plains 10, 12
polar bears 22

scorpions 20
sea 24, 26
sharks 26

# Wild animals quiz

What have you learnt about wild animals? Answer these questions and find out!

- Who does an elephant calf live with?

- Where do gibbons live?

- Which animal lives in the Arctic?

- Do dolphins live alone or in groups?

# Tick the books you've read!

## Level 2

Big Machines | Camping Trip | THE ANGRY OWL | Beauty and the Beast | Chicken Licken | The Monster Next Door | The Gingerbread Man | Wild Animals | School Bus Trip

Little Red Riding Hood | Nature Trail | Sports Day | Pirate School | Rumpelstiltskin | Sleeping Beauty | Don's Dragon | Superhero Max | TREEHOUSE RESCUE

Sly Fox and Red Hen | The Tale of JEMIMA PUDDLE-DUCK | The Three Little Pigs | Why Lion ROARRRS! | Topsy and Tim The Big Race | Town Mouse and Country Mouse | Topsy and Tim Go to London

## Level 3

Puss in Boots | ANGRY BIRDS MATILDA SAVES THE DAY! | Sharks | Thumbelina | Aladdin | YOU won't like this present as much as I DO! | The Elves and the Shoemaker | Hansel and Gretel | Harry and the Bucketful of Dinosaurs

Jack and the Beanstalk | Fury on Music Island | Poppet Stows Away | Rapunzel | The Red Knight | The Jungle Book | Roxy and the Great Escape | ANGRY BIRDS BOMB'S BEST BIRTHDAY | ANGRY BIRDS CHUCK!